MY VERY FIRST SIMBA STORIES

CAVE SECRET

Written by Ellen Weiss   Illustrated by Robbin Cuddy

DISNEY PRESS

FIRST EDITION
1 3 5 7 9 10 8 6 4 2

Library of Congress Catalog Card Number: 99-067855
ISBN: 0-7868-3265-7

For more Disney Press fun, visit www.disneybooks.com

DISNEP'S

MY VERY FIRST SIMBA STORIES

CAVE SECRET

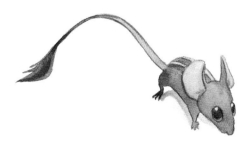

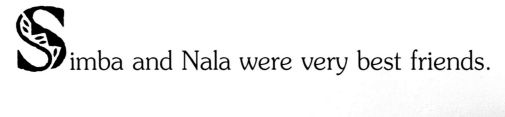

Simba and Nala were very best friends.

They liked to splash in the water hole, and sneak up on bugs, and race through the high grass.

And they liked to tell each other secrets—secrets that nobody else could know.

"I'm a little scared of mice," Nala told Simba. "Don't tell anybody."

"I'm scared of the dark sometimes," Simba told Nala. "Don't *you* tell anybody."

"I won't *ever* tell," said Nala.

"Me neither," said Simba. "I promise."

One day, Simba and his father, Mufasa, were out for a walk.

"Look at that little mouse stuffing her cheeks with seeds," said Mufasa.

"That's so funny!" said Simba. "I don't know why Nala's scared of mice."

"Nala is afraid of mice? That *is* funny!" Mufasa said.

At that moment Nala was just on the other side of the hill, chasing butterflies. She heard every single word.

Later, when she and Simba were together, Nala gave him a good hard whack.

"You promised not to tell!" she said angrily.

"You promised! And now your father knows, and he'll tell everybody, and they'll all laugh at me! That's the last time I'm going to trust you with a secret!"

"I'm sorry, Nala! Please don't stop trusting me!" Simba begged her. "I'll never tell one of your secrets again."

"Well . . ." said Nala, "we'll see."
Nala didn't stop playing with Simba, but
she did stop telling him secrets.

ut one day, a few weeks later, Nala finally changed her mind.

"I'm going to tell you a secret," she told Simba. "But it's a really big secret. And if you tell this time, I'll be so mad at you, I won't be friends with you anymore."

"I promise!" said Simba.

"Okay," said Nala. "Here's the secret. I found a really good cave yesterday, down in the red cliffs. But I was with my mother, so I couldn't go in. I'm going back to explore it today."

"Can I come with you?" Simba asked.
"No, it's my cave. I want it to be just mine,"
she said. "Maybe you can some other day."
And off she went to explore her cave.

Simba played all day without Nala. A little before dinner, he began to wonder when she was coming back.

Nala's mother was wondering, too. "Simba," she asked, "do you know where Nala is?"

"—No," he answered. He could not look her in the eye. It was the first time he had not told a grown-up the truth.

Now the sun was starting to go down. Simba was really starting to worry about Nala. Where was she?

Nala's mother was pacing back and forth, searching the Pride Lands with her eyes. "Where could she be?" she kept saying.

Simba wanted to tell her, he really did. But he had promised to keep Nala's secret.

The moon was rising.

Nala had never stayed away by herself for this long. Now the whole pride was worrying about her.

Sarabi, Simba's mother, came to him.

"Simba," she said, "do you know anything about where Nala is?"

"—I can't tell," said Simba. "It's a secret."

"A secret? What kind of a secret?" asked his mother.

"A big secret. I can't tell, no matter what!" Simba told his mother about how mad Nala had been when he'd told Mufasa she was afraid of mice.

"Simba," said his mother, "you're a good friend to try not to tell Nala's secret. But there are some secrets that are good to keep, and others that are important to tell."

"How do you know the difference?" cried Simba.

"If you think about it," said Sarabi, "you know in your heart if something is a good secret or a bad secret. This one is a bad secret. Nala might be in trouble somewhere."

Simba thought about what his mother had said. And he knew in his heart that this was a bad secret. He had to tell where Nala was.

He pointed across the Pride Lands to the red cliffs. "She's over there," he said. "In a cave."

Sarabi hugged her son. "I know it was hard to tell," she said. "But you were right to do it. Now, let's go find Nala."

The whole pride hurried across the grasslands to the red cliffs.

"Nala!" called her mother. "Naaa-laa!"

There was only silence, and the cry of the hyenas.

"Nala!" her mother called again.

They heard a small voice. "M-mother?"

They rushed to the place where the voice was coming from. It was the entrance to a cave, but it was almost completely blocked. A rockslide had tumbled down and trapped Nala!

They dug and dug, and finally the rocks were cleared away.

Out Nala tumbled, and ran to her mother. She was all covered with dirt.

"Nala! I was so worried about you!" cried her mother. "How could you do that?"

"I'm sorry!" said Nala. "I was so scared! I'll never go off without telling you again!"

Simba could hardly face his friend. "I'm sorry I told your secret, Nala," he said. "Please don't be too mad at me."

"Mad at you?" said Nala. "If you hadn't told, maybe nobody would have ever found me! That was a stupid secret, and I'm glad you told it!"

They walked home by the light of the moon. Nala stuck very close to her mother.

At bedtime, Nala and Simba snuggled together. "I'm so happy to be home!" she said.

"I'm happy you're home, too," said Simba. "And that's not a secret!"